Cross-eyed Lefty and the Steel Flea

Fabulous Novellas

Cross-eyed Lefty and the Steel Flea
by
Nikolai Leskov

Translated from the Russian by
Isabel Hapgood

Skomlin
House of Memory

Skomlin
House of Memory and Imagination
For more information visit *www.skomlin.com*

A Skomlin Book
Melbourne, Australia

First published in in 1881
First English version, Boston 1916
© Skomlin, 2017

ISBN: 978-0-6481826-5-8 *(paperback)*
ISBN: 978-0-6481826-6-5 *(eBook)*

 A catalogue record for this
book is available from the
National Library of Australia

The paper used in this publication meets the minimum requirements of ANSI/NISO Z39.48-1992 (R1997) (Permanence of Paper). The paper used in this book is from responsibly managed forests. Printed in the United States of America, the United Kingdom and Australia by Lightning Source, Inc.

CHAPTER THE FIRST

When Tsar Alexander Pavlovich had finished with the
Vienna Council[1] he got the idea of travelling about
Europe to see what the different countries had to show
him. He went to many countries, was very friendly and
had heart-to-heart talks with all sorts of people; they all
had something to impress him with and win him over
to their side, but he had with him a Cossack from the
Don, Platov[2] by name, who did not like all these goings
on; Platov was homesick for his farm on the Don and
kept worrying the Tsar to go back to Russia. Whenever
Platov saw the Tsar getting interested in something foreign, with all his following standing by in silence, he
would go up to him and say, "That's all right, of course,
but ours at home are just as good." Then he would get
up to some trick to distract the Tsar's attention.

By the time the Tsar got to their country the English had heard all about this and they thought up some
pretty tricks calculated to capture his fancy by their
very foreignness and so take his mind off the Russians.
In many cases they succeeded, especially where there
were big assemblies and Platov could not say what he
wanted to in French. As a matter of fact he was not interested in French, for he was a married man and thought
all French talk too trifling to bother his head about. The
English invited the Tsar to their warehouses and arsenals
and soapworks and everywhere else to show that they
were so much better at everything than the Russians and
were thus able to boast. Then it was that Platov made
up his mind:

---

1 The Vienna Congress, September 1814-June 1815
2 Matvei Ivanovich Platov (1751-1818), a famous ataman of the Don
Cossack army, a popular hero during the Napoleon wars of 1812-1815.

"That's enough. I've put up with it so far but—no more! Even if I can't talk French I'm not going to let our people down!"

No sooner had he said this to himself than the Tsar spoke to him:

"You and I are going to see their arms museum tomorrow," he said. "They have many things of great perfection there and once you've seen them you'll stop arguing when you hear it said that we Russians "are no good at anything."

Platov did not answer the Tsar, he merely buried his big ugly nose in his shaggy cloak and went back to his quarters. There he ordered his batman to get a bottle of Caucasian vodka out of his hamper, knocked back a full glass, said his prayers before a travelling shrine, rolled himself up in his cloak and snored so terrifically that none of the Englishmen in the house could get any sleep.

"I must sleep on it," he thought.

CHAPTER THE SECOND

The next day the Tsar went to the museum with Platov; he could not take any other Russians with him because the carriage they gave him was a two-seater.

They arrived at a huge building with an indescribable entrance, corridors without end, rooms one after another, and, in the middle of the last big room, where there were all sorts of big busts, there stood a statue of the Apollo Belvedere under a canopy.

The Tsar kept glancing at Platov as they walked along to see whether he showed surprise and to find out what he was looking at. But Platov strode along with his eyes fixed on the floor as though he wasn't looking at anything at all and kept twisting the end of his moustache into a ring.

The English immediately started showing them all kinds of marvels and explaining what things they had for use in wartime: naval barometers, camel-hair cloaks for the infantry, and waterproof cloaks for the cavalry. The Tsar was very pleased with all this, everything seemed so good to him, but Platov was still waiting, nothing of this meant anything to him.

"How can you be like that?" said the Tsar. "Why don't you say something? Isn't there anything here that impresses you?"

And Platov replied:

"There's only one thing that impresses me: my Cossack boys fought without any of this and drove twelve nations out of our country."

The Tsar said:

"That's all prejudice."

To which Platov replied:

"I don't know what it's called, but I don't dare argue and must keep my mouth shut."

But the Englishmen, noticing the dissension between them, took them straight to the statue of Apollo Belvedere and took a Mortimer musket from one of his hands and a pistol from the other.

"Look," they said, "what we can make," and handed the musket to the Tsar.

The Tsar did not show any great interest as he looked at the Mortimer musket for he had some like it at Tsarskoye Selo, so they gave him the pistol and said:

"This pistol is of unknown, incomparable make—one of our admirals snatched it from the belt of a pirate captain at Calabria."

The Tsar examined the pistol and couldn't take his eyes off it.

"Oh," he gasped in amazement. "It is—how can anyone possibly do such wonderful work!" And he turned and said to Platov in Russian, "If I had just one such craftsman in Russia I would be very happy and proud and I would make that craftsman a lord on the spot."

When he heard that, Platov put his right hand into the pocket of his. big, baggy trousers and pulled out a gunsmith's screwdriver. The Englishmen told him that the thing didn't open but he paid no attention to them, and picked at the lock. He gave the screwdriver a turn or two and pulled the lock out. He showed the Tsar the cocking piece that had an inscription on it in Russian: "Ivan Moskvin in the town of Tula."

The Englishmen were surprised and nudged each other:

"Oho, we've been had."

But the Tsar said sadly to Platov:

"Why did you have to upset them; I'm sorry for them now. Let's go."

They got back into their two-seater carriage and drove off. The Tsar attended a ball that day but Platov knocked back a still bigger glass of Caucasian vodka and slept the sound sleep of a Cossack.

He was glad he had upset the English and brought the Tula craftsman to the Tsar's notice, but one thing vexed him: why had the Tsar felt sorry for the English under the circumstances?

"What has made the Tsar sorry for them?" Platov wondered. "I can't understand it at all."

Thinking deeply about this he got up twice, crossed himself and drank vodka until he forced himself to fall sound asleep.

The English couldn't sleep either because they were just as worried. While the Tsar was having a good time at the ball they got such a new marvel ready for him that even Platov's imagination was staggered.

CHAPTER THE THIRD

Next day, when Platov went to say "Good morning" to the Tsar, the emperor said to him:

"Tell them to harness up the two-seater and we'll go and look at some more museums."

Platov even made bold to ask, "Haven't we had enough, looking at foreign things?" he asked. "Wouldn't it be better to get back home to Russia?"

But the Tsar said:

"No, there are some more new things I want to see: they've been boasting about the first-class sugar they make."

Off they went.

The English showed the Tsar what fine goods they made and Platov kept looking at them and then said:

"Show us some *Molveaux* sugar from your factories."

The Englishmen didn't know what Molveaux was. They whispered and winked at each other and kept repeating, "*Molveaux, Molveaux*" and didn't realize that it's a kind of sugar we make in Russia and they had to admit that they had all the sugars there are, but no *Molveaux*.

Platov said:

"Then you haven't got anything to boast about. Come and visit us and we'll treat you to tea with real *Molveaux* from Bobrinsky's factory."[3]

But the Tsar tugged at his sleeve and said softly:

"Don't you go upsetting my politics."

3 Y.N.Molveaux's sugar refinery was near St. Petersburg and that of A. A. Bobrinsky in Tula Gubernia.

Then the English invited the Tsar to see the very last of their museums where they have minerals and insects gathered from all over the world, from the biggest pyramid of Egypt down to the tiniest flea that can't be seen with the naked eye but gets under the skin and bites.

The Tsar went there.

They looked at the Egyptian pyramids and mummies and-when they were leaving Platov thought to himself:

"Thank God everything went oil all right—there was nothing there to astonish the Tsar."

But when they reached the very last room they saw there workmen in sleeved waistcoats and aprons holding a tray on which there was nothing.

The Tsar was surprised at their offering him an empty tray.

"What does this mean?" he asked, and the English workmen said, "This is our humble gift to Your Majesty."

"But what is it?"

"Can you, please, see that speck?"

The Tsar looked and sure enough there was the tiniest speck of dust lying on the silver tray.

And the workmen said:

"If it please Your Majesty, lick your finger and take it in your hand."

"What do I want a speck of dust for?"

"It isn't a speck of dust: it's a flea."

"Is it alive?"

"Oh, no, it's not alive," they said, "it's made out of pure English steel, we forged it in the form of a flea and inside there's clockwork with a spring. Be kind enough to turn the key and it'll do a dance."

The Tsar was curious and asked:

"Where's the key?"

And the English workmen said:

"The key's there, in front of your eyes."

"Then why is it I can't see it?" asked the Tsar.

"That's because you need a microscope."

They brought a microscope and the Tsar saw that there really was a key lying on the tray next to the flea.

"Be pleased to take it on your hand," they said, "there's a special orifice in its belly; you turn the key seven times and it will begin to dance...."

The Tsar could hardly get hold of the key, with difficulty he held it between finger and thumb and took the flea between the thumb and finger of his other hand; as soon as he put the key in he felt its whiskers wiggling, then it began to move its feet and at last it gave a sudden jump, cutting a caper as it flew through the air; after that it did two variations on one side and two on the other and so on until it had danced a full quadrille of three movements.

The Tsar immediately ordered that a million be given to the Englishmen in any money they liked, silver five-kopek pieces or in small banknotes—anything they wanted.

The Englishmen asked for silver as they had a poor opinion of banknotes; then they showed another cunning trick of theirs: they gave the Tsar the flea but there wasn't any box to put it in and he couldn't keep either the flea or the key without a box as they'd soon get lost and thrown out with the dust. The workmen had made a case out of a whole diamond as big as a nut with a place for the flea carved out of the middle. But they didn't give him the case, they said, because it belonged to the

Exchequer and the English were strict about such things and they couldn't give it away even to the Tsar.

Platov got all worked up over this.

"What's all the swindling about?" he said. "You made the Tsar a present and got a million for it and that's still not enough for you! You always get a box with everything you buy."

But the Tsar said:

"Don't you go upsetting my politics. You leave matters alone; it's not your business. They have their own customs," and he asked, "How much does the nut cost, to put the flea in?"

The English asked another five thousand for it.

Tsar Alexander Pavlovich said, "Pay them," and himself put the flea in the nut and the key together with it and in order not to lose the nut put it in his gold snuffbox which he ordered to be placed in a travelling casket all inlaid with mother-of-pearl and whalebone. The Tsar took leave of the English workmen very graciously and said:

"You are the first craftsmen in the world and my people can do nothing to beat you."

They were very pleased with this and there was nothing Platov could say to contradict the Tsar. He only took the microscope and without a word slipped it into his pocket, for, he thought, it should go with the other things and, besides, they had paid out enough money as it was.

The Tsar knew nothing about this till they returned to Russia, and they left very soon, for the Tsar had turned melancholy on account of the war business and wanted to go to the Priest Fedot[4] in Taganrog to confession.

4 Author's Note "Priest Fedot" is not just taken out of the blue: the Emperor Alexander Pavlovich, before his death in Taganrog, confessed to the Rev. Alexei Fedotov-Chekhovsky, who afterwards called himself "His Majesty's Confessor" and liked to make much of this purely accidental occurrence. This Fedotov-Chekhovsky is apparently the legendary Priest Fedot.

There was little pleasant conversation between them on the road for their minds were filled with different ideas: the Tsar was of the opinion that the English had no equals for skill but Platov insisted that our people could make anything they saw, only they hadn't had the proper training. He put it to the Tsar that the English workmen had different rules of life for everything, for science and for general living, and that every man had excellent opportunities for everything so that things had a different meaning for him.

The Tsar didn't want to listen to too much of that sort of thing and Platov, seeing that, didn't press him. And so they travelled in silence and at every station Platov would get out to drown his vexation in a big glass of vodka and nibble a salt biscuit; then he would light his huge briar pipe that held a pound of Zhukov tobacco, after which he'd get back in the carriage and sit there beside the Tsar in silence. The Tsar would look one way and Platov would stick his pipe out of the other window and let the wind carry the smoke away. In this way they reached St. Petersburg, but the Tsar didn't take Platov with him to the Priest Fedot.

"You aren't fit for spiritual conversation," he said, "and you smoke too much, my head's full of soot from your pipe."

Platov remained behind offended and lay down on his couch and sulked and smoked Zhukov tobacco all the while.

CHAPTER THE FOURTH

The remarkable flea of English blue steel remained in Alexander Pavlovich's whalebone casket until he died in Taganrog having given it to the Priest Fedot to hand over, to the empress when she had sufficiently recovered. When the empress saw the flea's capers she smiled at them but didn't do anything else with it.

"Mine is a widow's lot," she said, "and nothing amuses me any more," and when she got back to St. Petersburg she handed it to the new Tsar with all the other valuables of his inheritance.

Emperor Nikolai Pavlovich did not at first pay any attention to the flea because of the disturbances when he ascended the throne,[5] but one day he began to examine the casket left him by his brother and got out the snuffbox, and out of the snuffbox came the diamond nut and out of the nut, the steel flea, but it hadn't been wound up for a long time and didn't work but lay there quietly as though it had gone stiff.

The Tsar looked at it and wondered.

"What rubbish is this and why did my brother take such care of it?"

His courtiers wanted to throw it away but the Tsar said:

"No, there must be some meaning to this."

From the chemist's opposite Anichkov Bridge they called a chemist who was used to weighing poisons on tiny scales and showed it to him and he put it on his tongue and said:

"It feels cold, like some hard metal." Then he tried it lightly with his teeth. "And if it please you, it isn't a real flea, it's a model, it's made of metal, and it's not our

5 The Decembrist Uprising in 1825.

handiwork, not Russian."

The Tsar immediately ordered that inquiries be made as to where it had come from and what it meant.

They hurried to look through records and registers but did not find any mention of it. They began asking one person after another, but nobody knew anything about it. Fortunately the Don Cossack Platov was still alive; he was even then lying sulking on his couch and smoking his pipe. As soon as he heard that there was such trouble in the palace he rose up from his couch, threw away his pipe and appeared before the Tsar wearing all his medals.

"What do you want of me, my brave old man?" asked the Tsar.

"I don't want anything for myself, Your Majesty," Platov made reply. "I have my fill of meat and drink and am satisfied. I have come to report about the insect that has been found. It happened in such and such a way," he went on to say, "and it took place before my eyes in England. There's a key to it and I have their microscope for you to see it through. If you take the key and wind it up through its belly it will jump as far as you like and do all sorts of dancing pranks."

When they wound it up it began to jump about.

"True enough, Your Majesty," said Platov, "it's a delicate and interesting piece of work but we mustn't let our admiration get the better of us; we must let our master craftsmen at Tula or Sesterbek" (Sestroretsk was called Sesterbek in those days) "have a good look at it and see whether they can't do something better so that the English won't be able to show they're better than the Russians."

Tsar Nikolai Pavlovich had great confidence in his Russian people and did not like to elevate any foreigner over them so he said to Platov:

"That was well said, my brave old man, and I will trust you to prove it. I don't need this box now. I've trouble enough without it, so you take it with you and don't lie on your couch and sulk any more but go to your quiet Don and have a heart-to-heart talk with my Cossacks there about the way they live and about their loyalty and anything else they would like. And when you pass through Tula show this insect to my craftsmen there and let them think about it. Tell them that my brother was impressed with it and praised the foreigners who made the insect very highly, but I rely on my own people and think they are no worse than any others. They won't disregard my words and will do something about it."

CHAPTER THE FIFTH

Platov took the steel flea and as he passed through Tula on his way to the Don showed it to the Tula gunsmiths, told them what the Tsar had said and asked them:

"What are we going to do about it, good folk?"

The gunsmiths answered:

"We, sir, are moved by the Tsar's gracious words and will never forget him because he has faith in his own people, but what we're going to do in the present case can't be decided in a minute, for the English nation aren't fools, either. They are quite clever, in fact, and their art has a lot of sense to it. To beat them," they said, "we have to think and ask the Lord's blessing. And if you, sir, have as much faith in us as the Tsar has, then go home to your quiet Don and leave us the flea as it is, in its case and in the Tsar's gold snuffbox. Have a good rest on the Don so that the wounds you received in defence of your country may heal, and when you go back through Tula stop here and send for us: by that time, God willing, we shall have thought of something."

Platov wasn't very pleased that the Tula people wanted so much time and hadn't said definitely what they hoped to arrange. He asked them this way and that, and chatted with them in the cunning manner of the Don Cossacks. The men of Tula, however, were no less cunning than he and they had immediately got hold of such an idea that they couldn't even hope that Platov would believe them and wished to put their bold plan into execution before they disclosed it.

"We don't know ourselves what we're going to do," they said, "only we'll put our trust in the Lord and we hope the Tsar will have no reason to regret his kind words about us."

Platov tried cunning arguments but he had met his match in the men of Tula.

He tried one artful move after another but when he saw that he couldn't get the better of them he handed them the snuffbox with the insect in it and said:

"There's nothing more I can do about it. Have it your way. I know what you're like, so there's nothing I can do but trust you, but you had better look out for yourselves. Don't try to replace the diamond and don't spoil the fine English work, and don't be too long about it because I travel fast. Before a fortnight has gone I'll be leaving the Don for St. Petersburg again, so be sure you have something for me to show to the Tsar."

The gunsmiths did their best to console him.

"We shan't spoil the fine work," they said, "and we won't replace the diamond. Two weeks is time enough for us and when you come back there'll be *something* for you to show the Tsar that is worthy of His Majesty."

But *what*, exactly, they were clever enough not to say.

CHAPTER THE SIXTH

Platov left Tula and three of the gunsmiths, the most skilled amongst them—one cross-eyed and left-handed, with a birthmark on his cheek, whose hair had been pulled out above his temples when he was serving his apprenticeship—took leave of their workmates and families, packed their bags, took some food with them and left the town without a word to anybody.

It was seen, however, that they did not leave by the Moscow Toll-Gate, but by the opposite one, in the direction of Kiev and it was thought that they had gone to Kiev to pray at the tombs of the saints or to seek the advice of the holy men always to be found there in large numbers.

Although this was close to the truth it was not the truth itself. Neither the time nor the distance would allow the Tula gunsmiths to walk three weeks to Kiev and after that do a job that would put the English nation to shame. They would have done better to go to Moscow to pray, since it was only "twice ninety versts" there and there were saints enough in the city. In the other direction it was also "twice ninety versts" to Orel but from Orel to Kiev was a good five hundred versts more. That was a journey they couldn't do in a hurry and if they had done it they would have needed a long time to rest, with their feet swollen and their hands trembling.

Some people even thought that the gunsmiths had merely boasted to Platov, had then thought better of it, got scared and run away altogether taking with them the Tsar's gold snuffbox, the diamond and the flea in its case that had caused so much bother.

But such a suggestion was quite groundless and unworthy of the craftsmen on whom the honour of the nation now rested.

CHAPTER THE SEVENTH

The people of Tula, clever people skilled in the art of metal work, are also well-known experts on matters religious. They enjoy this fame not only in their own country but also at holy Mount Athos: not only do they sing well, putting in all the trills, but they know how to paint the picture *Evening Bells*, and if any of them dedicate themselves to service and join a monastery they become famous as stewards and make the most skilled collectors of funds. At holy Mount Athos it is known that the men of Tula bring in the best results; if it were not for them the dark corners of Russia would probably never have seen many of the holy relics from the distant East, and Athos would have been deprived of much evidence of Russian generosity and piety. The "Athos Tulans" carry the sacred relics all over the country and are clever enough to collect funds even where there is nothing to collect. Your Tulan, then, is devoted to the church and is a great religious practitioner, so that the three gunsmiths who had undertaken to give their support to Platov and all Russia had made no mistake in leaving for the south instead of going to Moscow. They had no intention of going to Kiev but to Mtsensk, a district town of their own Orel Gubernia where there was a "graven stone image" of St. Nicholas that had come floating down the River Zusha on a stone cross in the most ancient days. That "menacing and terrifying" icon was a life-size depiction of the Saint in silver robes and with a dark face, a temple in one hand and in the other a sword called "Victory in Battle." The whole secret of the business was in that "victory": St. Nicholas in general, and the Mtsensk Nicholas in particular, was the patron of commerce and war and so, as gunsmiths, they went to pray to his icon. They held a service before the icon itself, another before the stone cross and returned home from there by night; without a word to anybody they set about their work in dead secret. They got together in Lefty's house, locked themselves in, closed the shutters, lit the lamp in front of the icon and began work.

They remained there a day, a second and a third; none of them left the house but all the time they were tap, tap, tapping away with their little hammers. They were forging something but what it was nobody knew.

Everybody was curious but nobody could find out anything for the workers spoke to nobody and did not show themselves outside the house. All sorts of people went knocking at the door with all manner of excuses, asking for a light or for some salt, but the craftsmen wouldn't open the door under any pretext; what they ate all that time, nobody knew. Attempts were made to scare them by cries that the house next door was on fire in the hope that they would run out and reveal what they were forging. Nothing, however, could trick the cunning gun-smiths. Once Lefty did stick his head and shoulders out and shout:

"Burn as much as you like, we're busy," and again slammed the shutter to and got on with his work.

Through chinks in the shutters it could be seen that a fire was burning and the people outside could hear little hammers ringing on the anvils.

In short the whole business was done in such great secrecy that nobody could find out anything, and this went on until the Cossack Platov returned from the quiet Don on his way back to the Tsar; all that time the gun-smiths spoke to nobody and saw nobody.

CHAPTER THE EIGHTH

Platov travelled with great speed and ceremony: he sat in his carriage and two Cossack orderlies sat on the box on either side of the coachman and belaboured him with their whips mercilessly so that he would keep going at a gallop. If either of the Cossacks dozed off Platov in his carriage would give him a reminder with the toe of his boot to speed up the gallop. So great was the effect of this method of encouragement that the horses could not be halted at any of the stations but always overshot the halting places by a hundred lengths. Then the Cossacks would reverse the operation with their whips and the coachman would drive back to the inn.

They entered Tula in the same way. At first they dashed a hundred lengths past the Moscow Toll-Gate, then the Cossacks operated on the coachman with their whips until he drew up at the inn and fresh horses were put in. Platov did not get out of the carriage but told one of the orderlies to bring to him, as quickly as possible, the gunsmiths with whom he had left the flea.

One of the orderlies ran off to tell the gunsmiths to come as fast as they could and bring with them the work that was to disgrace the English, but before he had gone far Platov sent more and more Cossacks to hurry them up.

He sent off all the Cossacks and then started sending people from the crowd of onlookers, and himself even put his legs out of the carriage in his impatience and wanted to run there himself; he ground his teeth with rage—they all seemed too slow to him.

In those days everything had to be done with speed and precision, so that not one minute should be lost that might be of value to Russia.

CHAPTER THE NINTH

The Tula craftsmen who were doing a wonderful piece of work were at that time just finishing it off. The orderlies ran, panting, to their destination but the people from the crowd didn't get far for they were not used to it and their legs gave way and they flopped to the ground and after that, out of fear of Platov, hurried home and hid wherever they could.

When the orderlies reached the house they called out loudly and as the gunsmiths didn't open the door they tried to break open the shutters. These, however, were strong and would not give, so they tried the door but that was held fast inside with an oaken beam. Then the orderlies took a log that was lying in the street, put it under the eaves the way firemen do and in a moment ripped the roof off that tiny house. They got the roof off but were knocked off their feet themselves by the foul air that burst out, for the gunsmiths had been working continuously in the little closed room and the atmosphere had become so thick that a man used to fresh air couldn't stand a single whiff of it.

"What are you doing in there, you so-and-so's, you bastards," the messengers screamed, "and how dare you make such a stink to knock us out. Isn't there any fear of God in you?"

The gunsmiths answered:

"We're just knocking in the last nail and when it's done we'll bring our work."

"He'll eat us alive by that time," said the messengers, "and leave nothing to remember us by."

But the gunsmiths reassured them.

"He won't have time to swallow you because we've

knocked in the last nail while you've been talking," they said. "Run and tell him we're coming."

The orderlies ran off, but they weren't too sure of things. They thought the gunsmiths might be deceiving them, so that they kept looking back as they ran; but the craftsmen ran after them and were in such a hurry that they had not had time to dress in a manner fitting the important person they were to appear before, but hooked up their coats as they ran. Two of them had nothing in their hands, but the third, Lefty, held the Tsar's casket in a green cover with the English steel flea inside.

CHAPTER THE TENTH

The orderlies ran up to Platov and said:

"Here they are themselves!"

Platov immediately turned to the gunsmiths.

"Is it ready?"

"Everything's ready," they answered.

"Let me have it!"

They gave it to him.

The horses were already harnessed, up and the coachman and postillion were in their places. The Cossacks had taken their places beside the coachman and were holding their whips over him in readiness.

Platov pulled off the green cover, opened the casket, took out the gold snuffbox and out of that the diamond nut. He looked at it. The English flea was lying there but apart from that there was nothing else.

"What's the meaning of this?" asked Platov. "Where's the work you wanted to please the Tsar with?"

"Our work's there as well," the gunsmiths answered.

"What sort of work have you done?" asked Platov.

"Why explain it?" said the gunsmiths. "It's all there in front of your eyes. You have a good look at it."

Platov shrugged his shoulders and roared:

"Where's the key to the flea?"

"It's there," they answered, "the key's where the flea is, in the same nut."

Platov tried to pick up the key but his short, stumpy fingers wouldn't hold either the flea or the key to its belly mechanism no matter how he tried, and he began to let out a stream of real Cossack profanity.

"You scoundrels haven't done anything," he shouted, "and you've probably spoilt the whole thing! I'll have your heads for this!"

"There's no need to insult us like that although we have to put up with it because you're the Tsar's envoy but since you doubt us and think that we are capable of playing a trick on the Tsar even, we shan't tell you the secret of our work; be kind enough to take it to the Tsar. He'll see what kind of people he has and whether he has cause to be ashamed of us."

But Platov screamed back at them: "You're lying, you scoundrels, but I'm not letting you go like that. One of you will come to St. Petersburg with me and there I'll make him tell me the secret."

With that he stretched out his hand, seized cross-eyed Lefty by the collar with his stumpy fingers so that all the hooks flew off his coat, and threw him down at his feet in the carriage.

"You can sit there like a poodle all the way to St. Petersburg," he said, "and you'll be responsible for all of them. And you," he said turning to his orderlies, "get a move on. Don't doze and see that I'm in St. Petersburg at the Tsar's palace the day after tomorrow."

The craftsmen dared only say on behalf of their work-mate that Platov shouldn't take him away like that without any paper because he wouldn't be able to get back. Instead of answering them Platov showed them his fist, a terrible, red, gnarled fist covered with ugly scars, shook it at them and said, "There's a paper for you!" And to the Cossacks he said:

"Off you go, lads."

The Cossacks, the coachman and the horses all worked

with a will and carried off Lefty without any papers and, in two days, as Platov had ordered, galloped up to the Tsar's palace at such speed that they flew past the columns.

Platov got out, put on his medals and went to the Tsar leaving the Cossack orderlies to keep watch over Lefty at the palace gates.

CHAPTER THE ELEVENTH

Platov was afraid to appear before the Tsar, for Nikolai Pavlovich was a man who noticed and remembered everything, and never forgot a thing. Platov knew that he was certain to ask about the flea. And he, who had never feared any enemy in the world, took fright: he went into the palace with the casket and quietly placed it behind the stove in one of the rooms. Once he had hidden the casket Platov appeared before the Tsar in his study and began his report on the heart-to-heart talks he had had with the Cossacks on the quiet Don. "I'll keep the Tsar *busy* with this," he thought, "and if he remembers the flea and talks about it I'll have to answer him, but if he doesn't say anything I'll keep quiet, and I'll tell the valet who looks after the study to hide the casket and Tula Lefty can go into a fortress where he can remain until he's wanted."

Tsar Nikolai Pavlovich, however, had not forgotten anything, and as soon as Platov had finished telling him about his heart-to-heart talks he straight away asked him:

"And what did my Tula craftsmen do that's better than the English flea?"

Platov answered what he believed to be the truth.

"The flea, Your Majesty," he said, "is just where it was and I've brought it back, but the Tula craftsmen couldn't do anything more wonderful."

"You're a brave old man," said the Tsar, "but what you've told me can't be true."

Platov assured him that it was, and told him the whole story of what had happened. When he got to where the Tula gunsmiths asked him to show the flea to the Tsar,

Nikolai Pavlovich tapped him on the shoulder:

"Bring it here," he said, "I, knew my people wouldn't let me down. They've done something that is beyond all understanding."

CHAPTER THE TWELFTH

They brought the casket from behind the stove, took off the cloth cover, opened the gold snuffbox and the diamond nut—and there lay the flea just as it had done before.

The Tsar looked at it and said:

"What the devil!" But his faith in his Russian workmen was not shaken and he told his people to call his favourite daughter, Alexandra Nikolayevna, and said to her, "You have delicate fingers. Take the little key and wind up the machine in the insect's belly."

The princess began to turn the key and the flea immediately wiggled its whiskers but its feet didn't move. Alexandra Nikolayevna wound it up as far as it would go, but the insect didn't dance and didn't cut any of the capers it did before.

Platov turned quite green and shouted:

"Oh, those dirty swindlers! Now I know why they didn't want to tell me anything there. It's a good thing I brought one of the fools with me."

At that he rushed to the palace gate, caught Lefty by the hair and banged his head back and forth until some of the hair came out. When Platov had stopped beating him, Lefty said:

"I lost enough hair when I was an apprentice, and I don't know why that has to be repeated now."

"I'll tell you why," answered Platov, "it's because I trusted you and vouched for you, and you've spoilt a rare piece of work."

"We are very pleased that you vouched for us," answered Lefty, "but we did nothing to spoil it: look at it under the most powerful microscope and see for yourself."

Platov ran back to tell the Tsar about the microscope but threatened Lefty in parting:

"And you, you so-and-so, I'll give you what for."

He ordered his Cossacks to tie Lefty's elbows back still tighter and as he ran panting up the stairs muttered a prayer to himself, "Oh, King of Kings, Oh, pure and holy Virgin...." and so on to the end. The courtiers standing on the staircase turned away from Platov for they thought that he was in trouble and would be sure to be kicked out of the palace, and they couldn't stand him on account of his bravery.

CHAPTER THE THIRTEENTH

When Platov told the Tsar what Lefty had said the Tsar exclaimed joyfully:

"I knew my Russian people wouldn't let me down," and ordered a microscope to be brought to him on a cushion.

In a moment it was brought in and the Tsar took the flea and put it under the glass, at first back upwards and then on its side and then belly uppermost, but whichever way he turned it he could not see anything. But still the Tsar did not lose faith and just said:

"Bring that gunsmith who is downstairs to me right away."

"He ought to be properly dressed," said Platov, "he's wearing what I took him in and he's rather tousled."

"It doesn't matter," said the Tsar, "bring him as he is."

Said Platov:

"And now, you so-and-so, you can go and answer to the Tsar yourself."

"So what about it?" said Lefty. "I'll go and I'll answer."

He went as he was: in battered boots, one trouser leg tucked into a boot and the other dangling, the hooks torn off his shabby old coat and the collar all in shreds: but he wasn't a bit worried about his appearance.

"What about it?" he thought, "if the Tsar wishes to see me I must go to him and if I haven't got any papers it's not my fault and I'll tell him how it happened."

As soon as Lefty entered and bowed, the Tsar said to him:

"What's the matter, young man, we looked at the flea this way and that and put it under the microscope and couldn't find anything worth talking about."

"Did it please Your Majesty to look well?" asked Lefty.

The courtiers signalled to him: that's not the way to talk; he didn't understand court manners, he couldn't talk with cunning or with flattery and spoke with simplicity.

But the Tsar said:

"Keep your wisdom to yourselves and let him explain as best he can." And he explained to Lefty:

"We placed the flea like this and like this and put it under the microscope. Look," he said, "yourself, you can't see anything."

"That way, Your Majesty," answered Lefty, "you won't see anything because our work is too fine for a thing of that size."

"Then how can I see it?" asked the Tsar.

"You must put one of its feet in full detail right under the microscope," said Lefty, "and look separately at each of the heels it steps on."

"Good Lord," said the Tsar, "that must be awfully small!"

"How can we help it," answered Lefty, "if that's the only way to examine our work? But you'll see something to astonish you."

They placed the flea as Lefty had said and when the Tsar had taken one look his face beamed. He took hold of Lefty just as he was, all dusty and unwashed, embraced him and kissed him and then turned to his courtiers and said:

"You see, I knew better than anybody that my Russians wouldn't let me down. Take a look, if you please, why, the rogues have shod the English flea's feet!"

CHAPTER THE FOURTEENTH

They came up one by one and looked: the flea had actually been shod on all feet with real shoes but Lefty said that that wasn't the most astonishing thing.

"If you had a better microscope that could magnify five million times," he said, "you would see that each gunsmith had put his name on the shoes he made so that you know which Russian craftsman made which shoe."

"Is your name there, too?" asked the Tsar.

"Oh, no," said Lefty, "mine's the only one that isn't there."

"Why?"

"Because my work was smaller than those shoes: I made the nails the shoes are put on with and that's something you can't see in any microscope."

"Where is your microscope," asked the Tsar, "the one you used to produce such a marvel?"

And Lefty answered:

"We are poor people and can't afford such things but our eyes are trained to the work."

Then the other courtiers, seeing that Lefty had come out on top, began to embrace him and Platov gave him a hundred rubles and said:

"Forgive me, brother, for pulling out your hair."

"God will forgive you," answered Lefty, "and we're

used to that sort of snow falling on our heads."

He did not say any more for he had no more time to talk to anybody: the Tsar ordered that the shod flea be packed up and sent back to England as a sort of gift so that the people there would know that it didn't impress us. The Tsar ordered a special messenger to take the flea, a man who knew all languages and ordered Lefty to go with him so that he himself could show the English what sort of craftsmen we have in Tula.

Platov made the sign of the cross over Lefty.

"May my blessing go with you," he said, "and I'll send you my own Caucasian vodka for the road. Don't drink too little or too much but just average."

He did as he promised and sent the vodka.

Count Nesselrode[6] ordered Lefty to wash himself in the Tulyakovsky public baths; he had his hair cut by a hairdresser and was dressed in the parade uniform of a court chorister so that he should look like a man of rank.

So they got him ready for the road, gave him tea with Platov's vodka to drink, pulled in his belt so that his bowels wouldn't be shaken up and carted him off to London. From there Lefty's foreign adventures began.

---

6 Count Nesselrode—Minister of Foreign Affairs and Imperial Chancellor.

CHAPTER THE FIFTEENTH

The Tsar's messenger and Lefty travelled very fast, without stopping to rest anywhere between St. Petersburg and London. At every posting station they pulled their belts up another hole so that their bowels wouldn't get mixed up with their lungs; since his presentation to the Tsar Lefty had been allowed, on Platov's orders, to drink as much vodka as he liked at state expense, and he. kept going on that without any food and sang Russian songs all the way across Europe, merely adding a foreign refrain:

Ai, luli, luli, C'est tres joli.

As soon as the messenger brought him to London he went to give the casket to the proper people, leaving Lefty in a hotel room, but Lefty soon got fed up there and, besides, he wanted something to eat. He knocked at the door and when the servant answered pointed to his mouth, and he immediately took him to the dining-room.

Lefty sat down at the table and didn't know what to do next—he couldn't say anything in English. Then he thought of what to do: he simply knocked on the table and pointed to his mouth and the English guessed he wanted to eat and brought him things, but not always what he wanted and he didn't accept what he didn't like. When they brought him a pudding made in their fashion and all in flames he said, "I don't know how to eat such a thing," and didn't touch it so they took it away and brought something else. He wouldn't drink their vodka, either, because it is green and looks as if it were mixed with verdigris. He took what seemed most natural to him and then enjoyed his bottle in the cool room as he waited for the messenger.

The people to whom the messenger had taken the insect immediately examined it under the most powerful microscope and sent a description to the newspapers so that it would be published next morning for everybody's information.

"And that craftsman," they said, "we want to see him."

The messenger took them to the hotel room and from there to the dining-room where our Lefty had already got a good load on, and said, "There he is!"

The Englishmen patted Lefty on the shoulder and shook hands with him as an equal,

"Kamerad," they said, "Kamerad, fine craftsman—we'll talk to you later on but in the meantime we'll drink your health."

They ordered a lot of wine and offered Lefty the first glass, but he politely refused to drink first: "They might want to poison me because I have them beat," he thought.

"No," he said, "that's not right: the host must drink first, then I'll drink."

The Englishmen tried all the wines before he drank and then began to fill his glass. He stood up, crossed himself with his left hand and drank the healths of all of them.

They noticed that he crossed himself with his left hand and asked the messenger:

"What is he, a Lutheran or a Protestant?"

"He's neither a Lutheran nor a Protestant," answered the messenger, "he's Russian Orthodox."

"Then why does he cross himself with his left hand?"

"He's left-handed, he does everything with his left hand."

This astounded the English still more and they began

pouring wine into Lefty and the messenger and kept it up for three whole days and then said, "Enough." They drank a siphon of soda water each and quite refreshed began to question Lefty: where and what he had learned, how far had he gone in arithmetic?

"Our learning," said Lefty, "is simple: we read the Book of Psalms and the Book of Half-Dreams but we don't learn any arithmetic at all."

The Englishmen glanced at each other and said:

"How very odd!"

"That's the way it is everywhere in our country," answered Lefty.

"And what sort of book in Russia is this Book of Half-Dreams?" they asked.

"It's a book about this: if there is anything about the reading of dreams that King David left unclear in his Book of Psalms, the Book of Half-Dreams gives additional explanations."

"That's a pity, it would be much better for you to know at the least the four rules of addition in arithmetic, it would be more useful to you than your Book of Half-Dreams. Then you would have known that every machine is calculated for a certain power and although you're very clever with your hands you didn't realize that a tiny machine like the flea is calculated with great precision and can't carry the shoes you put on. That's why the flea doesn't jump or do dances any more."

Lefty agreed with that.

"There's no arguing about that," he said, "we're not very strong in learning but we're loyal to our country."

The Englishmen said to him:

"Stay here with us. We'll give you a good education and you'll become a wonderful craftsman."

To this, however, Lefty did not agree.

"I have parents at home," he said.

The Englishmen offered to send money to his parents but he wouldn't take it.

"We are attached to our country," he said, "and my father's an old man and my mother's an old lady and they're used to going to church in their own parish and, anyway, I'd get bored here all alone because I'm not married."

"You'll get used to it," they said, "accept our faith and we'll find you a wife."

"That can never be," answered Lefty.

"Why not?"

"Because," he said, "our Russian faith is the true faith; our ancestors believed in it and so must we."

"But you don't know our faith," said the Englishmen. "We have the same Christian beliefs and we have the same Gospel."

"The Gospel is truly the same for all," said Lefty, "only our books are thicker than yours and our faith is fuller."

"What makes you think that?"

"We have everything to prove it," he answered.

"What proofs have you?"

"We have these: we have icons created by God, we have others that weep and we have holy relics, but you have nothing. You haven't even got any church festivals except Sunday, and the second reason is that it would be embarrassing for me to live with an Englishwoman even if we were lawfully married."

"Why should it be?" they asked. "Don't look down on our women. They dress very neatly and they're good housewives."

But Lefty said:

"I don't know them."

"That doesn't matter, you'll get to know them; we'll arrange a rendezvous for you."

Lefty felt ashamed.

"Why trouble the girls for nothing?" he said and refused them. "A rendezvous is for gentlemen and doesn't become us, and if they heard of it at home in Tula they'd make real fun of me."

This made the Englishmen curious. :

"If you don't have a rendezvous," they asked, "how do you manage to make sure of a good choice?"

Lefty explained to them how we do things.

"When a man wants to make known his intentions towards a girl," he said, "he sends an old woman, a matchmaker, and she makes the proposal, then they go together to the girl's home and see her publicly, in front of all her relations."

They understood what he had told them but said that they had no matchmakers and no such custom but Lefty said:

"So much the better, for to do anything of the sort one must have honourable intentions and as I don't feel well disposed towards a foreign nation why should I trouble the girls?"

The Englishmen approved of his opinions and again patted him on the shoulders and knees very affably and asked:

"There's something we want to know out of curiosity: what faults have you discovered in our girls that you're so anxious to avoid them?"

Lefty answered that question quite frankly.

"I don't want to find fault only I don't like the way their clothes billow around them and you can't tell what they've got on and for what purpose; here she has something and underneath it there's something else pinned on and she has some sort of stockings on her hands. And their velvet talmas are like those they put on little monkeys."

"How does that hinder you?" asked the Englishmen, laughing.

"It's no hindrance, only I'm afraid I'd feel ashamed watching her and waiting till she gets out of it all."

"Can it be that your fashions are better?" they asked.

"Fashions in Tula are simple," he answered, "each wears her own lace and even the great ladies wear our lace."

They showed him their ladies, poured him out tea and asked:

"What are you turning your nose up at?"

"We're not used to anything so sweet."

So they gave him a piece of sugar to hold in his mouth, Russian fashion.

They thought that would be worse but he said:

"To our taste it's better."

The Englishmen couldn't do anything to make him fancy the English way of life; they could only persuade him to be their guest for a short while during which time they would show him their factories and their skill in making things.

"And then," they said, "we'll take you in one of our own ships and *bring you alive to St. Petersburg.*"

To that he agreed.

CHAPTER THE SIXTEENTH

The English took Lefty under their own protection and sent the Russian messenger back to Russia. Although the messenger was a man of rank and knew different languages, they were not interested in him, but in Lefty, whom they took round and showed everything. He saw all their metal factories and their soap factories and he liked them; he liked the way things were done and especially the way the workers lived. Every worker had enough to eat all the time and wasn't dressed in rags but in a good sleeved waistcoat and thick leather boots with iron tips so that he wouldn't hurt his feet if he trod on anything; he didn't work from fear of the whip but had been properly taught and understood what he was doing. The multiplication tables hung in front of every worker and to hand he had a slate: whenever a craftsman did anything he looked at the multiplication tables and checked what he was doing with understanding. Then he would write something on the slate and rub something else out and got everything right; whatever was written in figures came out in the work. And on holidays they'd gather in couples, walking sticks in hand, and walk along sedately, in proper style.

Lefty had a good look at the way they lived and at their work but he paid the greatest attention to something that astounded the English. He wasn't so interested in the way they made new muskets as he was in the condition of the old ones. He would look at the new guns, praise them and say:

"We can make them as well as that."

Whenever he came across an old musket he'd stick his finger in the muzzle, run it round the walls of the barrel and say:

"That beats ours by a long shot."

The Englishmen couldn't make out what Lefty had got his eye on.

"Could you tell me whether our generals have seen this or not?" he asked them,.

"Those that were here must have seen it," they told him.

"And were they wearing gloves or not?" he asked.

"Your generals are always in full dress," they told him, "and always wear gloves so they must have worn them here."

Lefty didn't answer. But he suddenly became miserable and terribly homesick.

"I thank you humbly for your hospitality," he said to the English. "I've been very pleased with everything and I've seen all I wanted to see, now I want to get home as quickly as I can."

They couldn't persuade him to stay any longer. They couldn't let him go overland because he didn't know languages and it wasn't advisable to go by sea as it was autumn and stormy, but he insisted: "Let me go."

"We have looked at the barometer," they said, "there's going to be a storm; you may get drowned, for this is the real sea, this isn't your Gulf of Finland."

"It's all the same where a man dies," he answered, "it's the will of God and I want to go home before I go off my head."

They didn't hold him back by force. They gave him food, provided him with money, presented him with a gold repeater watch as a memento and a woollen coat with a hood to protect him from the cold at sea. They dressed him very warmly and placed him on board a ship bound for Russia. They gave him the best cabin, like a real gentleman, but he didn't want to sit below decks with the other gentlemen but went up on deck, sat down under a tarpaulin and asked:

"Where is our Russia?"

The Englishman he asked would point in the direction with his hand, or indicate it with his head and Lefty would turn his face that way and gaze impatiently in the direction of his native land.

When they sailed out of the bay into the open sea his longing for Russia grew so great that he could not be consoled. The tossing was terrible but Lefty didn't go down to his cabin, he sat under his tarpaulin, pulled his hood down and stared towards home.

Many times the English tried to take him down to a warm place but he lied to them so that they would leave him alone.

"No," he said, "I'm better up here. If I go down under the roof I'll get seasick."

All the time he didn't go below except for an important reason, and this was to the liking of a certain English skipper's mate, who, to Lefty's sorrow, could speak Russian. This sailor was greatly surprised that a Russian landlubber could stand all that bad weather.

"Good boy, Russ!" he said. "Let's have a drink."

Lefty had a drink.

"Another," said the mate.

Lefty took another drink and they both got tipsy.

The mate asked Lefty:

"What's the secret you're taking back to Russia from our country?"

"That's my business," answered Lefty.

"If it's that way," said the mate, "then let's make a bet, English fashion."

"How?" asked Lefty.

"We bet never to drink alone but always together and the same drink; and whoever outdrinks the other wins the bet."

"The sky's cloudy, my belly's rowdy, I'm bored to death, there's a long way left, and I can't see my home for the waves—the bet'll make me cheer up a bit," thought Lefty to himself.

"All right," he said, "it's a go."

"But play fair,"

"Don't worry about that," said Lefty.

They agreed and shook hands on it.

CHAPTER THE SEVENTEENTH

Their bet began in the open sea. They kept on drinking till they reached the Riga Dunamunde keeping perfectly level, neither falling behind the other, and so well matched were they that when one of them looked at the sea and saw the devil creeping out of the water, the devil would immediately appear to the other, except that the sailor saw a red-headed devil and Lefty saw one that was dark, like a blackamoor.

"Cross yourself and turn away," said Lefty, "that is the devil rising out of the deep."

The Englishman argued with him:

"It's a diver."

"If you like," he said, "I'll chuck you into the water and you needn't be afraid, he'll give you back to me at once."

"If that's so you can chuck me into the water," said Lefty.

The Englishman picked him up and carried him to the rail.

The other sailors saw them and stopped them; they told the captain and he ordered them to be locked in a cabin together and that rum and wine and cold food be given them so that they could keep their bet—he didn't give them hot pudding with flames because it might set fire to the spirit inside them.

So they were brought safely locked up to St.Petersburg, and neither of them won the bet and in port they were laid out on different carts and the Englishman was taken to the English Embassy on the English Quay and Lefty to a police station.

From then on they suffered greatly different fates.

CHAPTER THE EIGHTEENTH

As soon as the Englishman was brought into the Embassy a doctor and an apothecary were sent for, the doctor ordered him to be given a hot bath in his presence, the apothecary there and then rolled a pill and put it in his mouth, then the two of them took and laid him out on a feather bed, covered him with a heavy coat and left him to sweat and gave orders that nobody in the Embassy should sneeze in order not to disturb him. The doctor and the apothecary waited until the mariner had fallen asleep, then they made another pill for him, placed it on the table beside his head and went away.

Lefty was dumped on the police station floor where they asked him:

"Who are you and where have you come from? Have you got a passport or any other document?"

On account of sickness, the drink and the tossing of the ship he was so weak that he did not say a word, but only groaned.

They searched him, took off his fine clothes, took away his repeater watch and his money and the police captain ordered him to be taken to the hospital free of charge in the first sleigh they could find.

A policeman took Lefty out to put him in a sleigh but it was a long time before he could find one, for sleigh-drivers avoid the police. All this time Lefty was lying on the cold, stone steps; then the policeman caught a cabby but the sleigh was without a fur rug for in such cases the cabbies hide the fur rugs under them so that the policeman's legs will get frost-bitten more quickly. So they took Lefty uncovered and transferred him from one sleigh to another, dropping him and picking him up again and pulling his ears to bring him round: They took him to one hospital but they wouldn't accept him without a document, so they took him to a second and a third and a fourth and so they kept on until morning, dragging him round all the distant alleys and byways and moving him from one sleigh to another until he was all beaten black and blue. Then a doctor's assistant told them to take him to the Obukhov Free Hospital where people of unknown origin were taken in to die.

They told the policeman to sign something and to sit Lefty on the floor in the corridor until they could deal with him.

In the meantime the English petty officer, since it was already morning, got up, swallowed the other pill, made a light breakfast of chicken and rice, washed it down with soda water and asked:

"Where's my Russian comrade? I'm going to look for him."

He dressed and went out.

CHAPTER THE NINETEENTH

In some amazing way the petty officer very soon found Lefty and they still hadn't got him to bed, he lay on the floor in the corridor and complained to the Englishman.

"There are a couple of words I must say to the Tsar," he said.

The Englishman ran to see Count Kleinmikhel[7] where he created a disturbance.

"How can you allow it? Hasn't he got a human soul under his ragged coat?" he said.

For this wise thought the Englishman was driven away so that he wouldn't dare mention a human soul again. Then somebody told him he ought to see the Cossack Platov, whose feelings were simple and human.

The Englishman found Platov who was back on his couch again, sulking. He listened to the petty officer and remembered all about Lefty.

"Why, brother," said Platov, "I know him very well, I've even pulled his hair, only I don't know how to help in this present misfortune because I've finished with the service and have quite retired. Nobody respects me any more, but you go to the Commandant Skobelev.[8] He has power and he's had this sort of experience so he'll do something for you."

The petty officer went to Skobelev and told him everything, what kind of disease Lefty was suffering from and how it had happened. Sikobelev said:

"I know that illness. Only the Germans can't cure it,

7 Count Kleinmikhel, Minister for Foreign Affairs, Imperial Chancellor under Nikolai I.
8 General Skobelev, a general under Nikolai J, for many years commandant of the Fortress of Peter and Paul.

what you need is a doctor from a priestly family, because they've known such cases from childhood and can help: right now I'll send you the Russian doctor, Martin-Solsky."

The only thing was that when Doctor Martin-Solsky arrived Lefty was already dying for the back of his head had been split open on the pavement and all he could gasp was:

"Tell the Tsar that the English don't clean their musket barrels with brick-dust; we shouldn't clean them that way, either, for if there should be a war, which God forbid, they won't be any use for shooting."

And with that expression of loyalty Lefty crossed himself and died.

Martin-Solsky immediately reported the matter to Count Chernishev[9] so that he should bring it to the Tsar's notice but Count Chernishev shouted at him:

"You look after your emetics and purgatives and keep your nose out of what doesn't concern you—there are generals in Russia for that."

So nobody ever told the Tsar and the muskets were cleaned that way right up to the Crimean War. And then, when they started loading the muskets, the bullets rattled in them because the barrels had been enlarged through being cleaned with brick-dust. Then Martin-Solsky reminded Chernishev of Lefty's words and the count said to him:

"You can go to hell, sawbones, and mind your own business, or I'll deny that you ever said anything of the sort to me and you'll get into trouble."

"He'll deny it, sure enough," thought Martin-Solsky and kept his mouth shut.

---

9 Count Chernishev, Minister for War and President of the State Council.

If Lefty's words had been conveyed to the Tsar in time things would have turned out differently during the war in the Crimea.

CHAPTER THE TWENTIETH

All this is now "a matter of days long past," a "legend of the days of old," but the days aren't so very old, either, so we need not be in a hurry to forget the legend, despite the air of fable it has about it and the epic character of the hero. Lefty's real name, like those of many of the world's greatest geniuses, has been lost for posterity; he is, however, interesting as a myth created by the fantasy of the people and his adventures can serve to recall a whole epoch that has here been precisely and faithfully rendered.

Needless to say, there are no craftsmen like the fabulous Lefty in Tula any more: machines have served to smooth out inequalities in talents and endowments and genius cannot do battle against industry and accuracy. Although machines favour an increase in wages they do not favour that artistic daring which, at times, broke down all barriers and which inspired the popular fantasy to compose legends like this present story.

The workers, of course, can appreciate the advantages they gain from devices put at their disposal by science but they remember the days of old with pride and affection. This is their epic and one with a very "human soul."

1881

www.ingramcontent.com/pod-product-compliance
Lightning Source LLC
Chambersburg PA
CBHW021939170626
46807CB00007B/3197